Tales of Chivalry

Compatible with

The 9th Age™

Impressum:

Written by the T9A Team

Published by FlorianGressConsulting, Rosenweg 24, 93053 Regensburg, Germany

Printed by Amazon Media EU S.à r.l., 5 Rue Plaetis, L-2338, Luxembourg

ISBN: 978-3-9824212-3-0

THE IX AGE
FANTASY BATTLES

A 9TH AGE SUPPLEMENT

KINGDOM OF EQUITAINE
TALES OF CHIVALRY

THE IX AGE
FANTASY BATTLES

A 9TH AGE SUPPLEMENT

KINGDOM OF EQUITAINE
TALES OF CHIVALRY

Faction leader: Peter G. Orfanos

Head of Background: Edward Murdoch

Contributing authors: Sebastiaan Follens, Charlie Lloyd, Henry P Miller, Edward Murdoch, Peter G. Orfanos, Glenn Patel, Matt Perriss, Alessandro Vivaldi, John Wallis, Calisson

Editing: Peter G. Orfanos, John Wallis

Linguistic support: Ghiznuk

Layout: Kacper Bucki

First Edition 05/2021

Dearest Abu Zafar,

As you travel upon this hopeful journey, I take this moment to offer counsel. Nephew, you move among exalted circles now. Your valiant efforts in the name of our newly recognised goddess, our blessed Lady, have brought you great accolades from the Motherland, and earned your invitation from His Majesty. Yet you are the first from our colony to travel to Equitaine since our accession, and this carries dangers.

I am certain King Henry will recognise in you the greatness of our people, and our place within the Kingdom shall be secure. But you step in a nest of sand vipers, and the slightest of missteps will see them poison the King's ear against you. You must use the time upon this journey to prepare, learn, know them as well as they know themselves.

I provide these collected scrolls as the best armour I might offer to you upon this quest. Bear it well, and do honour upon our ancestors. Our titles may mean little to the Vetians now, but in time, they will know us and our worth.

Go in peace and may success meet your steps.

Mansur al-Hafiz

—Letter sent to Equitaine's newest Duke, from the colony of Tawat en-Unser.

HISTORY

The Battle of Camavon, 836 A.S. Eugène Deladame, oil on canvas, 102 x 78"

Eugène Deladame (804 – 869) was a notable painter of the Avrantic period in the Destrian and Aeturian schools. *The Battle of Camavon* is an early work; it commemorates the famous military engagement, traditionally dated A.S. 9, when the rebel knight Uther "defeated" the mighty Gilles de Raux, Prime Necroprince of the Deathless Realm and Eternal Lord of the Greater Mysteries. Uther was subsequently crowned first mortal king of Equitaine.

The style exemplifies Avrantic tendencies towards exaggeration and emotionality, the fires of battle illuminating the human hero as he stands atop the body of his headless foe. The historical Uther, of course, hailed from a rather remote and unimportant dukedom of northern Equitaine, and there is no evidence he achieved anything of note until he joined the army of the Sunsword Saint and profited greatly from her glory in the East.

Similarly, the artist panders to traditional Equitan propaganda about the new king's status as a champion of the Lady, despite spending most of his early life consorting with foreign powers. There is nothing in contemporaneous accounts to suggest that the Green Knight was present at Camavon, as the artist depicts, or that a shimmering fleur-de-lis spontaneously appeared on Uther's shield.

Indeed, celebrated though Deladame's work has been, the best scholarship suggests that he was woefully misled by common mythologisation of the most important moments in Equitaine's history. Records show it is the Once and Future King Gilles who deserves the true credit for building the nation; he who saved the scattered peoples of Regio Equitatem from the Vermin hordes, who forged them into a single kingdom, who founded the knightly traditions and long kept the peace across the land, allowing the country to flourish for centuries before Uther was born.

For a fairer and more honest interpretation of the reign of Gilles the Deathless, we recommend the free thinker to visit Péricault's *Triumph of the Black King,* which hangs in the Hall of Ceremonies.

> —*Plaque accompanying a painting shown in the Guênac headquarters of the Weaver's Guild, a gentlemen's club and fraternal society with lodges throughout western Vetia.*

SOCIAL CASTES

My sisters, my loves, my dearest hearts,

Long has the realm been governed by and for the three estates, given to us by Her will, and kept in sacred covenant since the time of Sainted Uther. In his wisdom, the first true king set forth how men should live and govern themselves. This he did to honor the strictures of the Queen of Cups and Her commands unto us: to be Brave, to speak True, and to Endure.

Thus since those days have we divided ourselves. Some are born of the earth, to toil and to serve. Others are born to battle and must bear arms and risk lives. The last are they that hear Her call and feel the stir in their breast that brings them to prayer and study. We must be exemplars of this third proud foundation stone. Heed well your studies, and be attentive to your teachers, for your minds must be as sharp as any knight's blade, and as swift as a yeoman's arrows. You will be more to your charge than a ward 'gainst black spellcraft; you will be his conscience and his life's guide.

When your studies here come to an end, they must continue wherever you go, for all the days of your lives. You will need this wisdom and you must continue to seek it out. Seek out what is True, for no wisdom comes from falsehoods. You must be a light in the darkness. You must uncover that which is hidden. You will need Truth to guide the clerics who will look to you for leadership. We must be their heart. We must guide their studies. Regardless of their oaths to King or Duke or Lord, it is to Damsels they put their faith, and we must be worthy of it. Seneschals, clerks, scholars, masons, and healers alike will look to you, as the Lady's own handmaidens, to know Her mind.

Those who pray and study, will in their turn serve both low and high-born alike. They will heal the sick, bandage wounds, recite prayers, teach the young, and advise all. And while they set to this task, it will be yours to look among them, both high and low, for those worthy to step outside their given state, and join an ordo. Seek those who have a quick mind and deep thoughts, as you also once were sought. Set them apart from their peers and offer them a place in the halls of learning, should their lord be able to spare them.

Beyond this, remember all the while that you must act as justice for the penitent. You must set their tasks, three times the weight of their sins, that they may return to their place in the world. They will seek you out to set their atonements and you must do so with great resolve. Give no light sentence, and remember that they may be set to your tasks, for when they serve you, they serve the Evermaiden Herself. Send them unto the dark places, upon quests most dire, have them test themselves that they may know their own worth, and come back heroes or not at all. To spare is to spoil.

Remember these words, carve them into your heart, and shape this world to Her fair will.

—Damsel Alize of the Clover Hill Schola

KNIGHTS

My son,

By the time you read this, you will be a knight. Your days as a squire at Lord Crispin's court are over – you are to return home with all haste and take up my duties as acting lord of our demesne while I am away on crusade. An abrupt and unceremonious end to your squiredom to be sure – usually one earns one's knighthood through worthy deeds, but sometimes necessity is our master. I am certain your future will contain enough worthy deeds for a hundred knights. In the meantime, I trust His Grace ensured you underwent the traditional rites – the sacred oaths, the night vigil and the last strike. Let this be the last time any man strikes you without consequence, for a knight suffers no dishonour.

I suspect you are disappointed at having such a pivotal event in your life conducted hastily in a small sanctuary before you are unceremoniously sent on your way. When I return, I shall tell you more of my ascent to knighthood – I was raised to the title on a cold winter night in a muddy field, surrounded on all sides by Åsklander marauders. Most of the squires raised alongside me had met their end before the sun had set on the following day. The honour of knighthood was one for which they were glad to lay down their lives. They received no praise nor lavish feast for their deeds. In many ways, they were truer knights than many who bear the title today.

Remember then, that a knight is not made by the opinions of others, but by his heart and his deeds. A man who craves glory and adulation without accomplishments to his name is no knight, but a vainglorious fool. In time, you will receive the honours you deserve, but first you must be tested.

Reflect on the oaths you swore in the months to come – to act in accordance with the sacred virtues of the faith. Strive to live by the knight's code. Many can name the Seven Principles: Excellence, Forbearance, Generosity, Justice, Valour, Honour and Faith. Yet as you likely know, there are many such lists, and the true qualities of knighthood cannot be so easily prescribed. Through a lifetime of ordeal and reflection, I have come to understand the knight's way thus:

Always speak the truth, for a life built on lies can only lead to ruin. Treat your fellows and the world with kindness and compassion as befits a knight, and you will win their respect and love. Be a shield to those who cannot defend themselves. This above all: be true to yourself, for you cannot then be false to other men.

To be courageous is to be strong, but true courage requires more than strength of arms. Find the inner strength to uphold your convictions, and the will to withstand the tribulations of a life on the knight's path. Oppose evildoers wherever you find them. Do not idly seek out quarrels, but should you find yourself in one, ensure those opposed to you beware. Be the sword of righteousness that falls only on those deserving the wrath of justice.

Shy not from ordeal. Display valour and mercy in war, and magnanimity in peace, and always uphold the faith. Defend our land and our people, even unto death. Should you falter on the path, seek redemption through good works and prayer. The balance between your duties as a lord and your knightly oaths is among the greatest challenges you will face in this life. No one possesses the qualities to fully succeed in such an endeavour. You will struggle and you will fail, and this is what makes us worthy. Redeem yourself in the eyes of the Lady, and become more than you were through your ordeal. Some are crushed by defeat, while others are made small by victory. Greatness lives in those who can travel both roads with grace.

The balancing act between your duties as a lord and the knightly principles is one of the hardest tests you will face in this life. One day, you may face a choice where you will have to discard a knight's honour for the general good of the realm. Have a care that you do not stray too far down this path of expediency before honour, as many false knights have done.

Protect and guide your sisters. Ensure the youngest are diligent in their studies. Gwenaëlle is as zealous and headstrong as ever – she will test your patience and thumb her nose at your newfound authority. Do not let her undermine you in your duties as lord, but do not judge her too harshly. Remember that the bonds of blood are sacrosanct, and family is all. I pray my letters to her will spare you the worst of her wrath.

The burghers of Bréval may petition you for rights to cultivate our northern territories, hoping to take advantage of my absence. Categorically refuse all such requests. The forests and lakes near the Perilous Vale are holy places, no less so than any sanctuary. Despoiling these sacred lands would be a grievous sin and would invite ruin for the selfish gain of the few. A delicate truce exists with the mercurial woodland fey who call those groves home. Do not underestimate their capriciousness. I will write more on this when I find the time.

By the Lady's grace, I give you my blessing. May we meet again after this war, and may we both be strengthened by our ordeals in the months to come.

Your father,
Lord Pelleas Giantsbane, Warden of the Lakes

—Letter discovered among the affairs of Lord Gawain,
Warden of the Lakes, upon his death at the age of 97

PEASANTS

It was too green. Too green for autumn. As green as childhood memories, as green as the first blush of spring. The grim pines of Volksingen had given way to a mess of crabapples that scarcely deserved the title, for when one landed in the coach, it was sweet as a honeycake.

I shook my head, and fought the reflex to make the sign of the stahl. I was coming home. Father had recalled me. For whatever reason, he had decided that he needed his fourth spare son, and so this was now home again. I would need to relearn customs and shackles I had thought I would never need again, become Equitan once more. Duty demanded it.

As the coachman drove us onwards, I watched the lands. I had left convinced my home was a provincial backwater, that I lost nothing of value by leaving it when Father had permitted me to go and find a path for myself: his odd, scholarly fifthborn. As I returned, my eyes sharpened by time away, I saw far more.

Young Olivier, I was sure it was he, was tending what had been his father's plot – and he was as tall as the students I had been living with. Robust, strapping, in the flower of health – he looked like he could snap Berfried or Frix in half. I would have disregarded him as an exception, save that I soon saw that he was no different to all the youth of these lands.

Not just the people, either. Ears of wheat a third again the size of those on Frix's estate. A bull the height of a horse. How could I have forgotten such a bounty? Arrogance, no doubt. The interests of commoners held no fascination for one such as I. Not then.

On my return, however, I studied them as intently as any wild specimen I had ever turned my sights upon. Their musculature was not surprising; Aschau had its barrel-chested labourers. No, what surprised me was their rude good health. Less poxy, less battered. The peasants worked industriously, stripping the fields bare as fast as a swarm of locusts. Nothing scientific, but well motivated. A hundred small plots, harvested faster than a dozen large ones, organised by a certain logic – for each family knew their land, had it in their bones.

The hamlet nearest my home helped dissipate my contempt for my past self. It was now the night before some festival or other, and the decorations were small and shabby compared to the towns and cities I knew. Garlands of flowers are ever beautiful, of course, but the ribbons were tired and faded, darkened by overuse. The furniture was rough and mismatched, lacking the simple elegance and uniformity of the great beer-hall benches the Sohnstahl commoners rode on nights of revel. For all their hard labour, they were impoverished in material goods, far removed from the great workshops and factories of the Empire – though to me they now seemed enriched in other ways.

Pondering wealth took my thoughts down a sorrowful path. I had studied economics, knew the tithes of serfdom were high – most of those bountiful crops were owed to my father and eldest brother for their protection. Certain battle scars told me that their bodies, too, had been offered up to their lord. There were no Berfrieds here, rising above their station. They were peasants now, and in all likelihood forevermore.

The night was dark, too, darker than the clear sky ought to make it, here in the shadow of the mountain. No fault of the people, to be sure, but my second home had glimmered with the promise of silver. My first skulked in the shadows.

Father didn't have much to say to me when he saw me.

"Your brothers are dead. You're my heir. Your sword lessons start at dawn."

Oh my.

—Diary of Cédric Blondeau, Baron of Thiers

CULTURE

Hélias,

You have to come to town! I know you said you wouldn't but I have news. The Ides Fayre isn't going to be a flop like last year; they've extended it all the way up to the Calends of Itre! There are traders and vendors from all over Gasconne on their way. His lordship is sponsoring melee and archery contests. And you know that Gaston will be set on stick fighting and gambling. There won't be another chance like this to win coin, and be seen! May Cyrde the Trickster be on our side for once!

There'll be at least three weddings too – the triplets Claudette, Laurette and Paulette, may the Merlord give their husbands-to-be strength. People are saying it's because Marquis Austin has come to a special arrangement with the Court of Troubadours.

Can you believe that? The Court of Troubadours, here in Acquebourg! He wasn't lying either – I've already seen Jolly Judoc and Richard Seven Skins in the market square, and Noll Lion-Throat in the common room at the Fox and Goose!

There are whisperings, too: they say the Minstrel King is dead. Poisoned by a rival, or maybe stabbed, or caught by bandits… They say he's the first Minstrel King to die undefeated in seven generations. This is going to be a huge celebration! The Fairfield Ordo has been ordered to triple the lambic and mead they had at last year's fayre, and a great hunt has been called by the Castellan!

We're all counting on you to come, brother. It won't be the same without you here to make us look intelligent.
Larquin

Azor,

Dearest cousin, you simply must attend father's fete on Whitewing's Sainted Day this year at the Februar Ides. It will be even better than the Sainted Zemire's Day carnival! I know the road is long to visit us, but I have so few girls my own age here at the castle, and I miss you terribly.

There will be squires from near and far, fair of face and testing each other at the tilts. There will be jugglers, mummers, acrobats, and troubadours to make my heart burst! Imagine, dancing with a handsome knight as the finest musicians in all the realm sign their songs of heartbreak or newfound love. Such a sweet ache, my stomach spins from it!

I must make offerings to Oob! May she ensnare a knight for me, with stature that towers a full cubit over other men, with slender waist and broad shoulders, and eyes that give a hint of the man's spirit and dignity.

And before you say it, father will not be as strict as last time! This year he must attend to important guests, and treat with his bannermen who have not seen him since last year's Sainted Day of Marmont the Younger. He may even take the field for the joust; we have heard that an old rival of his has declared his intent to enter. Father won't speak of it, but he grinds his teeth at the name, Nivelle. Should we do anything short of setting fire to the stables, Father will surely have no notice of us!

Sweet cousin, dear cousin, best of friends, and sweetest of hearts, say you'll come!
Vassile

Revelers, friends, travellers! Traders, clergymen, and of course, the Acquebourg town guards, who do such wonderful work keeping the vagrants out of your pockets – so you still have something left for the Castle!

The Court of Troubadours, by the generosity of the magnanimous Marquis Austin of Bremont, invites you today, gathered in numbers this town has rarely seen before, to witness an event the likes of which your grandparents never saw, and likely not their grandparents either: The Tourney of the Witless!

You see, The Court of Troubadours has suffered a peculiar tragedy of late. Our esteemed leader, King Corentin the Bright, has been recalled to the Lady's tender care. I know, many of the ladies will mourn him greatly, as do I.

But, fear not! We courtiers will never allow such a holy duty as your entertainment to be held hostage to the whims of life and death! No, for we have gathered for you no less than twenty-seven of the challengers defeated by King Corentin at every tourney across the land during his long and celebrated career. They will compete for your favour, and you, the people of this fine country, will decide who shall be next to wear the Crown!

You will be dazzled by feats of physical daring, enthralled by songs fit for the Lady Herself – and maybe a few we'd best hope She doesn't hear! – and entertained in ways you had ne'er imagined 'ere this day.

But before we allow ourselves to get too excited, let us first remember His Majesty, the First Troubadour. Please, welcome The Witless and company, as they perform for us the Deeds of Minstrel King, on this, the Ides Fayre of Sainted Whitewing!

—"Lady" Camille des Rosiers, at the Duke's Head tavern, Acquebourg

POLITICS

The Count of Courbet: Your Grace, it is the honour and the privilege of the court to advise the King as he weighs the many burdens of the Crown. You are but lately come to the throne, and still in the first flower of your youth, so I hope you will permit me a short span to muster what eloquence I can concerning the subject here at hand.

Allow me to begin with a consideration of our nation's illustrious history. Every child of Equitaine knows the kingdom was established by our first and greatest hero, Uther, when he freed the lands from the Black Tyranny. But few remember that Uther did not fight alone. After the dead were driven from our castles and strongholds, he ruled over a court of noble allies and courageous knights, who aided the King in their stewardship of the realm.

Much later, the House of Uther finally passed from history, heirless. The terrible Wars of the Lily ensued, and proud Equitan blood was spilled. Afterwards, kings found it was wisest to rule in the example of the Lady's champion, by sharing power with the lords, relying on their strength and nobility to keep the peace, supporting them as they in turn support the Crown. There is no strength in solitude – only in allegiance.

Likewise, as Uther was ever faithful to the Lady, so have all good kings harkened unto the words of her Damsels. Thus it is that the history and fortune of the kingdom has been guided by the holy crusades called in Her name, the heathen lands captured for Her glory and for the prosperity of the Fair Realm. As you are all too keenly aware, our latest endeavour in Avras was betrayed by the villain General Fontaine, who has made himself a petty puppet King in that far-off city. But such infamy is the cruel exception to the rule of Equitaine's noble star as it rises around the world.

For you see, Your Grace, the wealth of foreign lands is eclipsed only by that of our own green country. Our fields, divinely blessed, are the envy of all Vetia – much of which, indeed, they feed. Our trading ships leave our southern ports for innumerable destinations, greatly enriching the growing burgher class. Our cloth and wine are just two of the peerless luxuries of the South, while in the North, shepherds guard fertile herds, and tame the mighty beasts we use in war.

This bounteous realm, vouchsafed unto us by the Queen Eternal, is worked by the sturdy peasantry, happy and secure in their place, serving and protected by the lords who in turn, as I have explained, uphold the King and ensure his rightful place upon the throne. It is an ancient and well-founded system, one that has served us all since Uther's day.

You see, therefore, why it is only right for our friend the Duke of Lauvon to request, in such humble, pious terms, this slight exemption from the royal tax, in memory of the ancient alliance between his seat and the Crown? I have no doubt that the King will act wisely in this matter, and the wise King would grant this boon for the sake of his liege lord, on whom the security of his very Crown in no small part depends.

King Henry: We thank thee, eloquent Courbet, for thy prudent and learned council. We know now how to proceed. Lauvon's tax shall be doubled for the coming harvest, and you, Courbet, shall serve the court no more.

You look surprised? Perhaps you were unaware that you are not the only student of history at the court. Yes, for we know how you served our beloved father, but lately laid to rest, filling his head with the council of submission, until you would have him stoop to kiss the boot of every petty landholder in the kingdom. And perchance you thought it had slipped our attention that Lauvon's only child is the fair lady wife of thy ignoble self?

Listen well, sons and daughters of Equitaine. We admire and affirm the proud lords of our realm. So long as our blood flows red, we will honour and uphold those who show their loyalty to our righteous Crown, but we will not cower before every snivelling, pitious demand for indulgence. For it is not just the lords but also the divine hand of the Lady who safeguards our nation and our throne. Recalling this, my friends, the court permits you to bring the next matter. Courbet is removed from our sight. Who will speak?

—Transcript of proceedings at the Court of Equitaine, 961 A.S.

NOTABLE INDIVIDUALS

PERCEHURE, His Majesty Henry, known as "the Young", King of Equitaine, son of Luis, grandson of King Charles, known as "the Strong"; b. 942; cr. 960; Beloved of the Lady of Silver Lakes, Protector of the Realm, Emperor of the Middle Sea, Master of the Maidens, Sovereign of the Chivalric Order of the Crown. Named King by popular acclaim, despite strong rivals in Duke Dumont and Earl El-Sylla. Responsible for declaring the successful invasion of Ascalon and the disastrous landing at Acrotère. Squire to Sir Guilhem. *Myraeum Lodge.*

LUPESCU, Her Highness Eleonore, daughter of Count Wladyslaw, known as "the Cunning", granddaughter of King Charles, known as "the Strong", b. 946. In the line of succession for the crowns of Zmayevatz, Equitaine and Sonnstahl. Known association with Princess Josefa of Sonnstahl, once presumptive heiress of the Empire. *The Sorcerous Academy of Zmayevatz.*

FONTAINE, General Robert, son of Briac Fontaine, Baron of Garderance; b. 907; servant of Sir Robert Mauldichat during the Arcalean Crusades of 947, stripped of all peerages and titles by King Henry in 960, due to Avras under his command seceding from Equitaine in 952. Took an Arcalean wife in 949, shortly after arriving in Avras. Is often known to invite her to attend meetings of state. Squire to Sir Robert Mauldichat. *Myraeum Lodge (frmr). Order of the Crown (frmr).*

AVELINE, Lady Hélène, daughter of Duke Dumont; b. 944; personal advisor on matters mystical to King Henry. Studied under Grand Dame Yseult. The youngest Damsel in a generation, still regularly attends her Ordo for continued study. *Ordo Fidem Gasconne.*

DUMONT, His Grace Armel; Duke of Gasconne, son of Duke Amaury, Commander of the Northern Fleet; b. 892. Companion and Bannerman to King Charles. Led the Second Crusade to Tawat en-Unser in 948. Had considerable support among Equitan noble families after Luis' failures. A strong traditionalist, he backed Henry for King citing the importance of continuity and lineage. Squire to Enguerrand de Bradbère. *Order of the Maidens.* Recipient of the Lady's Cross for Gallantry.

EL-SYLLA, His Lordship Rida, Earl of Marcabe, son of Earl Javar, grandson of Sheikh Nazmi El-Sylla; b. 931; Commander of the Taphrian Banners. Had considerable support among colonial nobles after Luis' failures. An ardent progressive, he backed Henry for King, citing the youthful energy Henry would provide. Squire to Corsablis Abou Jamel. *Order of the Middle Sea.*

FERET, Lady Tania, Knight of Port Reynaud; b. 917; originally from northern Taphria, knighted by Sir Richard Drayton, after a controversial duel. Served time in banishment, before being recalled to Court, answering the call to battle against the Black Tooth warherd. After the death of Luis, she impressed the new king, and was appointed Minister of War in 960.

MORTIMER, Sir Tristram, Knight of the Old Forest; b. circa 939; former bandit, pardoned and knighted by Duke Guichard d'Harmont after heroics in the campaign against barbarian incursions along the eastern border. Commands many of the finest archers in Equitaine, known for surprise warfare. *His Majesty's Cantemont Gaol (frmr).*

WYNCALL, Sister Alienor, Sister in the Ordo Academia Cantemont, daughter of Sir Wolstan de Mingen; b. 907. Refused entry to the Ordo to study the sciences, accepted instead to study music. Within the Ordo, became the first woman to expand into theology, then mathematics. Has made considerable contributions to the field in Equitaine, frequently consults on projects both in warfare and architecture. Her creation of the treadwheel crane has revolutionised masonry in Equitaine. *Ordo Academia Cantemont.*

GWAREDFELL, Holiness Eliaz; b. 919. Renounced all claims to title upon acceptance of his role under King Charles. Known for pursuing causes upon the word of the lowliest subject. Rooted out the Sightblinder Cult in Puremoor in 954. Slew Baron Garret Saincler in single combat after the testimony of offences against a peasant washerwoman were found to hold true. Current whereabouts unknown, save to King Henry. *Paladin of the Realm.*

> —*Selected excerpts from Pratt's Peerage, the leading authority on the etiquette and lineage of the noble families of Equitaine. "We help you know your Dukes from your Viscounts, your arms from your alms, and your Peerage from your pannage".*

HERALDRY

As we sat in the stands, the Ambassador leant over and explained to me, "The Knights of Equitaine place great importance on their heraldry. More even than the nobility of Great Sonnstahl."

He paused as the two knights in bright trappings crashed together in a violent collision of splintering wood and clamouring armour.

"There are three basic features," he continued. "The field colour denotes the knight's affiliation or origin, forming a background for the device. For instance, my dear Sir Amaury Desforges, who has unceremoniously unhorsed his opponent, is a knight of the House of Gasconne. The field of that dukedom is 'gules' – red. Even a peasant may bear a simple colour – called an 'ordinary' – to show allegiance to their lord or fiefdom, but it's important for knights to go somewhat further."

"See there: the other denotations are more personal, forming a complete coat of arms. They are passed down through the family line or expanded to demonstrate individual achievements."

The cheering crowd subsided, and Sir Amaury passed his unblemished shield over to the herald for display.

"The white arrow?" I asked in reply.

"Yes," spoke the ambassador. "Many emblems use a chevron, a stripe, a cross, or a division of sorts. In this case the 'chevron d'argent', meaning a white or silver arrow pointing upwards."

"And what about the more intricate designs?" The ambassador had piqued my curiosity.

He nodded towards the King's banner. "The Young King has taken up the 'lion d'or' – the golden lion on the gules field. It is a symbol of his authority and power. Fitting for an aspiring leader, don't you think?" I nodded my assent and he continued. "The lion he inherited from his father, King Luis, along with the red field. The Kings of Equitaine have long been riding to war under the Lion Banner. The golden colour he took from his mother's family's coat of arms. A shrewd political move to be sure, one to show kinship to the people of Port Roig. An essential trading port in Destria from which his mother hails. Lastly, the chalice was added upon his coronation. A sign of his divine right to rule."

After we stood for the ovation, he continued. "See the silver chain beneath the banner? It bears the tokens of his achievements, which we call charms. They are commonly displayed by knights below the shield or pennon, and are often blessed, sacred or even magical."

"What about Sir Amaury and his coat of arms?" I wondered aloud. "In addition to the field gules, the chevron argent, I also see three boars' heads, one either side of the arrow's tip and one below the chevron?"

The ambassador paused for a moment.

"I do believe he likes to hunt wild pig."

—Diary of Niklas Scheller, friend of Ambassador Tischendorf

THE THREE VIRTUES

Oh old lady of the spring, how can we achieve Glory? We live in a remote province; the ordo and our Lords forget us; we are eager to fight. Tell us how to pursue Ordeal, Honesty and Courage.

Oh children, like every young squire, you must understand Faith, first and foremost. It is easy to wish to fight, but fulfilling the hopes of the Lady is not. You are eager to pursue glory and the tales of others, but it's not to fulfil your pride that you should fight. The greatest Ordeal is inside you, not against the world. The highest Honesty is with yourself, not with others. The purest courage is in the smallest action, not in the most famous. Your duty is to forge your own way, not to follow the path of others.

Oh wise woman of the spring, how can we achieve the hopes of the Lady, if not through glorious battle? Our families told us of deeds of greatness, of slaying monsters and vanquishing the enemies of Equitaine, yet what if we cannot go to war on the farthest fringes of the world? How can we understand our own path?

Oh young squires, your path is your story. You should be eager to forge your tale, following your mind, your heart and your hand: for only they can fulfil and understand the nature of Beauty and the beauty of Nature. Your hands are Ordeal, your hearts are Honesty and your minds are Courage. Keep them pure and clear, and your story will be forged by the will of the Queen of Heaven.

Oh dearest mistress of the spring, please tell us of the Beauty of Ordeal!

Atonement is the Beauty of Ordeal. Look at your venerable Master at Arms. He is the oldest and dearest of my friends. Everyone, from the lords of our lands to the most respected of your families, forgot his name, and nonetheless he is still serving the Maiden Above – and our people. He committed the worst of sins; but he made atonement for them, and he served me, he protected me, he loved me like I was the Lady Herself. Unknown, his deeds forgotten… and nonetheless, there's no other master I would give you. For Ordeal means to fight within yourself to overcome the adversity of your own story, your own family, your own faith.

Oh mistress, what is the Beauty of Courage, which guides minds and deeds?

It is with Courage that your tale shall begin, for you cannot reach atonement and Ordeal without first confronting your sins. Don't lie to yourself. No one will tell you what Courage is, for sometimes it is the bowing of your head, sometimes it is the raising of your fist, and always it is listening to the voice of the Lady of Green Boughs within yourself.

Our dearest lady, what of the Beauty of Honesty?

Look at this spring. Its water is clear and filled with trout, a fish that lives only in the purest water. But the very same water will reach villages and cities, absorbing dirt and becoming populated with carp who love muddier waters. Nonetheless, all that unclean water will reach the sea and become pure again. There's no Beauty without atonement, and there's no atonement without sin. Many are lost seeking only pure waters. Honesty demands we recognise all parts of our nature; that we do not tell ourselves we are trout if we are truly carp. No one can understand atonement if they lack Honesty, and truly see the course of both pure and muddied water.

—The Litany of the Spring, a scripture kept in the Sanctuary of Rausère.

RELIGION

Interview Transcript – Inq First Class Dieter Werner
Subject: Halfling ("Roger")

958 AS, November 36th

Inquisitor Werner: What can you say of your time in Equitaine?

Roger the Halfling: Your worship, I never lived anywhere with better luck, better crops, or better wine… then again I've never known anywhere where so few of your kind last to old age. But that's what so much magic gets you – it's great stuff but there's such a thing as too much. As the Equitan say, the brightest candles cast the deepest shadows.

IW: You made mention that you've been employed at their religious houses.

RH: Yes, your worship, I worked in an ordo in Sague, the Thornapple Brotherhood, as it were.

IW: How long did you serve them?

RH: A span of eight years, or near enough, 'til the itch to wander needed a scratch.

IW: What is their organisational structure like? How much autonomy, how much sway over their Lords and Dukes?

RH: They advise mostly; some lords listen more than others. The ordos lean on noble patrons, for protection mostly and coin for the bigger projects. But the lords lean on the ordos too, needing them to pray for 'em, and 'cause the commoner folk listen to 'em. Each beholden to each, like husband and wife. It's like everything in Equitaine, really. Everyone serves someone.

IW: Everyone? What of the king?

RH: Him more'n all: his Grace serves the people, and is suitor to the Lady herself. So by law, must serve her too.

IW: I see… Tell me about them, is it true that their witches lead their church?

RH: Oh aye, your worship, but not like here, as it were. Day to day, it'd be an abbot, or chalicier, or some other official, as you like. Each of the ordos is different, each with its own traditions. Some are healers, others scholars, some fight. Some breed the animals, some keep books, some oversee construction of bridges, makin' of war machines, or buildings and the like. Ordos also brew the best beer, beggin' your pardon, better than the local stuff here by my reckon. As to the Damsels, well, they wouldn't say it as such, but they're near worshipped – "venerated" the word they use.

IW: I take it these Damsels are of the ruling class then?

RH: Beg pardon, your worship, but no. See, the ordos teach. Villagers, nobles, merchants, it makes no never mind. If they find a bright girl, a clever one, they send missive to the Schola, that bein' the name what the Damsels call their meetin' places. It's reckoned a great honor if one is chosen and taken to the Schola. Out in the secret places, they're real hidden like… no one knows what they do or how they're initiated, but everyone reveres them when they come back. That's probably why most chosen are nobles' daughters, but they'd be right offended if you pointed it out.

IW: Intriguing… tell me more. Everything you know.

RH: Well, they're like a high priestess, as it were. The small folk call them prophetesses. They can talk to the Goddess, so everyone shuts right up when they give a pronouncement – but they keep their own council most times. When they do speak out though, their people hear it like it were the Lady Herself tellin' them what for. And that's what they do, they advise when it's needed, and most other times they let the ordos run themselves.

IW: What do they do with all that free time I wonder...

RH: Oh aye, your worship, I can shed some light on that. I know how they spent some of their time, as I was tasked by them on a great many things. They have servants, rogues and warriors of all kinds, ones who don't work for no lord whatever. The small folk call them Quin, and say they follow some old trickster god – Sharr, Clever Cyr, Old Cut... too many names to remember – but they're no strangers to sword work, I can tell you that. See, the Schola have secret libraries, and the Damsels use any means to fill 'em. They go lookin' for old books, and tablets, and artifacts. What they can't buy, they have these Quin get for 'em. If the Quin don't work, well, let's just say they got the ear of the lord to whisper in. And it's not like the Equitan don't like a good Agurenne.

IW: An Agurenne?

RH: Oh right, you folks don't have a word for it here. It's like struggle, maybe suffering, or ordeal. It's more than that though. It means to strive or go after with all your heart.

IW: That says a great deal about them... Tell me, why do they restrict the teaching of spellcraft? Is that what the Schola do? Find and hide away lore?

RH: Oh my goodness gracious no. Fact is, the Equitan have more magic than near on any other people I've met. It's just the bigger spells they keep under key. They have these small magics, they call them orisons. They're little prayers, mixed with spells, that the ordos teach. I could never get the hang of it meself, but they could do a great deal with 'em. My friend, Rock, she could tie three knots in a string and find you any lost thing that could fit in hand, like it could guide her right to it.

IW: That doesn't sound like an Equitan name. 'Rock' was it?

RH: Short for Rachelle, she was a peasant girl, easy on the eye, had a habit of throwing rocks at me. Not that I deserved it much, your worship.

IW: Wait... Even their peasants are taught this?

RH: Aye, they're an odd people. Some things, the prophetesses say nay, and no one so much as ever asks about it again. Other things are allowed by anyone. Orisons are like that. Blessings they call them. Little gifts from the Queen of Cups herself.

IW: Like their accursed 'Blessing'? Is this where they get their protection which our magisters are unable to unravel?

RH: I can't rightly say, your worship. Could be that. Or could be how they stamp prayers on every ring on the best maille shirts. Could be the hymns they carve or burn into their shields. Could be the Charms they carry or the Fey Gifts. Could be psalms they recite on their way to a fight. Could be that every sword is anointed in the service of their faith. Or it could be all the praying that the ordos are paid to do all year long. Three times a day at the least. It's unending I tell you.

IW: I see… and what of their celebrated knights? The Sainted, I believe they're called? Are they part of the ordo?

RH: Yes your worship, those who finished the Quest, Grail Knights, Sainted, the Holy Few, many names for everything in Equitaine. But no, they ain't part of the ordos, the ordos follow them.

IW: The Quest?

RH: Aye, the Quest. Once in an Equitan's life, they're expected to do a great service or journey for the Fey Lady. Some take that a step further. They swear to take up Her Quest and renounce the world. It's a hell of a thing. They live in service to others, travel far and wide, and take every obstacle and challenge before them like it was sent by the goddess Herself. They renounce the world and do Her will as they see it. They claim that folks on the Quest get dreams and visions as to what to do, and where to go. They give up status, privilege, money, anything they had. I think the vow is that they 'need place themselves twixt those in need and the evils of the world.' Oh and folks take it real serious like. Show a lot of respect for those on the Quest, so they do.

IW: How is half that country not in shallow graves then?

RH: Like I said, your worship, it's not like everyone takes up the Quest, even if all are allowed. Most don't. Even those that do can give it up after three years of proper Agurenne. No shame in coming home after giving your best, as they say. And it's hard to find Her.

IW: Find who?

RH: Her, the Keeper of Keys. She of Lake and River. The Evermaiden. That Her. Their Goddess, like. She tests them and tests them. Sometimes for years and years, but they say at the end, the Mistress of Stone and Stream Herself comes to find *them*, and bid them drink from Her own cup. Drink from Her own chalice, and they change. I've seen them. The Sainted. Words don't do justice, your worship. Half mortal, half divine to my eye, radiant. The Equitan worship them more than they do the prophetesses. They swear by them, name things for them, treat their words like holy teachings. Should they fall in battle, even their bones are worshipped. And just being around them makes miracles and magic happen. I've seen it.

IW: I can see you believe that.

RH: That I do sir. Old Roger does not lie, and I'll do you good and honest service, just as I did in Sague for them of the ordo there. I like working in churches and temples and holy places, something calming about it. Best be about it soon though – our caravan moves on next month, and it's a long old road to Pontefreddo.

IW: Very well, you shall have my recommendation. Just a few more questions…

SAROLDE

In days of olde, times rarely told, there lived the honoured Maid Sarolde;
Against the lords of blood and night, she fought afore the King foretold.
When Uther still was but a youth, with much to learn of Lady's truth.
Then good Sarolde did rise and lead, drive all to fight with nail and tooth.

Most humbly she was peasant born, and gaily weathered noble scorn;
'Gainst chain and yoke she turned her wrath, rebellion on her shoulders bourne.
To the undead they took the fight, advancing under bright sun's light;
Believers to her banners flocked, to help refute Death's false birthright.

Yet flames can only blaze so long, and men can only stay so strong;
Sarolde's brave band betrayed and caught, defiance lost to all but song.
In fair Gasconne a monster dwelt, a savage Count to whom all knelt;
Her comrades held in deepest cell, their torment she most grimly felt.

A plan she formed against the threat, a legend none would soon forget;
Her life she'd trade to end the strife, ensure her people free were set.
She knew Death's mind; pride would compel, to show his sin in citadel;
To common serfs he paid no care – they'd help Sarolde prepare his knell.

Black tar and oil in pyre's foundation, they placed there for Death's sure damnation;
The spark awaited soon was lit, and fire did spread across the nation.
And so Sarolde goes to her end, and never once do her knees bend,
She speaks last words for all to hear: of end to Night her cry portends.

A dozen vampires gathered nigh, their ashes soon cast to the sky.
The villain and his kin all slain, undone by mortal strength allied.
That day the Maid of Gasconne burned, and evil all its wages earned.
Her story told to every child; to Equitaine she hope returned.

—From the Lay of Light, a collection of poems and legends widely distributed throughout Equitaine.

GEOGRAPHY

Many have heard my tales of travel and adventure, yet I am often asked about the lands of my home. It is time I showed them to the wider world, beginning with this humble guide for the newcomer.

The crusader ships in the harbour of Cantémont – the pilgrim's (and merchant's) gate to the Middle Sea – are protected by impressive cliffs. The underwater caves make a wonderful howling sound that gives the city its name. From here, one can explore the dry southern realm of Hausère, with its hills of vineyards, olive trees and grazing sheep, its central floodplain dominated by Entragues, a city known for its Arcalean-influenced craftsmen and free-thinkers (at least, free by Equitan standards!).

The capital city, Guênac, is an inland harbour built on an island in the Guêon river. Here, one finds not just royalty and courtiers, but also religion. The King's Keep serves as the base of operations for the Paladins, and many other ordos maintain a presence in the city. The famous Dome of Glass covers perhaps the largest and most magnificent of Equitaine's "sanctuaries" – a type of circular, museum-like holy building often found on an ordo's estate, housing historical accounts, artwork and sometimes relics.

Following the river downstream, one discovers the fertile abundance of Ciélac, the breadbasket of Vetia, arriving at Jovigny-le-Pont, known for its remarkable lifting bridge and the many fine villas nearby, where noblemen come for hunting and good weather. Make sure to visit in the month of Damos for the huge midsummer festival, featuring the most important jousting tournament in the kingdom!

Up the northwest coast, one arrives in Brezann, mysterious land of magic and misted hills. The largest settlement in this sparsely-populated region is the humble fishing town of Morcuse, with its lighthouse guiding the way into a "Hidden Sea", where merpeople dwell in the waters and pegasi soar in the sky. Throughout this realm, you will find strange creatures and enchanted sites, such as the lake of Calpéron, high in the hills, said to grant visions from the Lady.

East of Brezann lie the hardy northern lands of Hengelaw, home of the Gasci tribe in ancient times, known for mighty woods, cold weather and tough draft-horses. One even sees Åsklander heritage in some parts – at the industrial port of Bradpole, for example. The region is more densely populated near the large city of Gasconne, home to "Uther's Seat", a rocky crag in the shape of a throne near the castle that overlooks the town, supposedly the origin of the Kingdom's founding hero. Today, the city is a center of finance, not to mention a thriving theatrical tradition where yours truly has been pleased to tread the boards!

It only remains to mention Sague, the wild heartland of Equitaine. With its untamed crags and endless forests, most travelers come here only to pass through to other lands – or else to hunt and tame the fabled beasts and chimeric creatures that dwell within. I myself have experienced extraordinary adventures in Sague, and have visited the dramatic castles of Corante and Charroque.

Of course, today the Fair Realm extends across the Middle Sea to the colonies of Taphria and beyond. I could tell you many a tale of the hot sun and swaying palms of Port Reynaud and other such destinations that draw both holy warriors and wayfarers like myself. Remember to find me when you have a penny to spare, my friends!

—From the pamphlets of Samuel le Pepin, professional pilgrim and storyteller.

WARFARE AND THE CRUSADES

Dearest Abu Zafar,

I know you were but a boy when the second crusade of the Equitans arrived at our gates, and the first occurred years before your birth. You have trained in the knightly practices, learned the chivalric virtues, and you are a rival to any man with lance and sword. You do honour to your father's memory, may his soul rest. Yet the spectacle of a true Equitan army, in all its might and glory, that is a thing you have still to witness. I shall provide the memories here of an old man, imperfect though they may be.

The oasis for which our city is named has long drawn those of a spiritual nature. We were no strangers to the occasional pilgrim from Vetia. Yet the first crusade to Tawat en-Unser took us all unawares. It had the appearance of a spontaneous mob, lacking in support, but the hundreds of crusaders and militants made for an impressive statement. The second crusade was a different beast altogether. Its approach was like a sandstorm from the Great Desert, seen in the sky long before its arrival. As your father's only brother, I commanded the Tawat forces through both wars. We called for aid from Taaj Abdullah and neighbouring sultans, but none came, for reasons political or strategic. Within the year, our walls had fallen, yet we had learned much of the invaders, and began to embrace their ways. Now, a decade later, we are truly a part of the Lady's people.

First, and truly foremost among the nation's armies, the Knights of Equitaine are a force of hoof and steel felt across the world. In numbers beyond the reach of all but a handful of global powers, steelclad heavy cavalry encircled our walls during the Second Crusade, driving off or killing our outriders and cutting off all routes of resupply. They rode knee to knee, row upon row of shining lances and colourful heraldry on show, a mastery of horsemanship and martial prowess.

In the weeks to follow, we came to know our foes to be more than competent soldiers. Even in the heat of battle, they attempted to follow strange codes of conduct. At times they would show mercy to the wounded or disarmed, demonstrate courage in the face of defeat, honour their word even to their cost and oft disciplined their own men as harshly as their foes. What we saw as a weakness in the early days, we came to recognise as the mortar which bound their army together, and the inspiration which drove them forward.

A less spectacular but still vital pillar of the war force, milites represent the lowborn elements of Equitan armies. Easy to underestimate those grubby collections of mismatched clothing and arms, but calloused hands and weather-worn faces belie the essential role they play. The levies of men raised by nobles from their estates provide much of the practical support for an army. Carrying supplies, digging earthworks, and holding ground when directed by the nobility.

Bowmen are a strength of the northern dukedoms, and we witnessed their power with the flurries of white fletched arrows which rained upon our walls during each sortie, together with crossbow bolts from the peasants of southern realms. With them rode yeomen on fleet mounts and bearing the heraldry of their masters; even among their peasants, the tokens of rank and fealty were apparent.

The ordos, under the guidance of Damsels, bring the Faith and the military together, though each ordo offers its own contribution to the machinery of warfare. In the days of the First Crusade, peasant crusaders made up much of the force arrayed against us. Ragged and disordered, armed with makeshift weapons and patched armour, they carried their belief like a torch in their eyes.

The Ordo Militant were no less devoted to their cause. Their quiet rhythmical prayers, back-breaking labour and weapons drills seemed endless, with not a moment wasted in indolence. By contrast, the Ordo Minister had none of their brethren's martial tendencies, yet their compassion and commitment were without fault – as was their bravery, walking the lines of battle, administering healing to friend and foe alike. I myself only survived the raid of the western fields thanks to their tender hands, when a lance took me in the chest and broke several ribs. Several months later, I was ransomed back to Tawat en-Unser in perfect health, and considerably more knowledgeable about the invaders.

The Ordo Academia offers the benefits of teachings passed down through generations, master to apprentice. In the end, it was their intervention which brought an end to hope of resistance against the Second Crusade. When the great trebuchets brought down entire sections of the city walls, and scorpions shattered our own defensive emplacements, we could no longer hold back the flood of knights entering the city. Our surrender followed, though as we would come to learn, it was only the beginning of a longer journey.

Irregulars are a difficult group to say anything precise about. No commander could rely upon them for a prolonged campaign, yet if they can be persuaded, cajoled or bribed into joining a battle, they can provide an edge beyond the experience of ordinary soldiers. Brigands are adept at striking without warning; arrows flashed from the forest around our oasis many times during and between the crusades. And the knights who have sworn a quest can be even more unpredictable. Fierce fighters, but their loyalties are always towards their own personal geas, as I would hear them describe their voyages. If it aligns with a general's goal, all to the good, but woe betide any who would stand in their way.

Then there are the Fey. Many years passed before I glimpsed them, though I knew the stories. In the months that followed the occupation of Tawat en-Unser, when the waters of the spring were purified and tended by those of the Faith, the grove took on a new quality – a tranquility I had not thought to experience before the grave. The first time I saw a naiad step from the water, I wept. It was like a dream, where beauty and peace filled my mind. I still hold the Alihat trinity in my heart, but now I've seen the Lady's glory, and I know they serve a role in Her Court.

Since that blessed day, I have had the fortune to witness the Fey's unpredictable behaviour many times. Their aid can rarely be guaranteed, yet once given, it can sway the tide of any battle. Ghostly knights to scythe through enemy lines, shapeshifting beings emerging from forest or lake to strike at weak points, purest unicorns bearing their riders through the thickest tangled branches.

Those you should watch for most are the Sainted, those noblest of mortals who have earned their place among the Lady's court, and now bear the mark of her service. Should you have the opportunity to befriend one, it would serve you most well. They are beyond petty politics, yet their word is all but law across much of the country.

May these words be of service to you.
Mansur al-Hafiz

STEEDS

My dearest Master Gerond,

I am arrived! The road from Aschau was long. I was discharged from my escort into the hands of the Duke of Sarbonne's men at the border, flattering me with false courtesy for the sake of my knowledge. Without it, I suspect they would not lower themselves to speak to one of such lowly birth.

But the horses! They are truly a breed apart, reared largely on the meadows of the South, the bloodlines ancient and fiercely guarded. I should have listened to you and taken the annual contract as you did so many years ago. The yeomen ride light-boned hotbloods, beautifully coupled in the hock, full of grace and yet such evident strength. Truly a prince among horses – and such speed! If we could gain a breeding stock, the Guild would never need for funds again.

And yet they are as nothing compared to the mounts of the knights. At least eighteen hands, and half again the musculature of a typical Ullsberg stallion. I am in awe of such a combination of power and poise. Each is worth a king's ransom, I am sure. The knights ride with extraordinary confidence – despite my inherent distaste, I cannot fault their horsemanship.

One of the yeomen described the skilled manner in which the horses are bred, backed and trained for war, a process that takes many years and brings rider and steed "closer than lovers", as he put it. Even the chimeric breeds are usually reared from birth – since a mature or even juvenile hippogriff, pegasus or peryton can only be brought to saddle by the most skilled and valient minds. It is evident that the mounts of Equitaine hold a unique and special place in its culture.

On the long ride to Sarbonne I inspected not just the stock but their tack and harness. While the leatherwork is fair, the ironwork is basic and the steel, while competent, is not extensively produced here. No wonder they tolerate our expertise, even if it is only once a year.

Your humble apprentice,
Mattias

Master Gerond,

I am penning these notes from a draughty stone-walled room in Castle Sarbonne, having spent three days forging bits and saddle trees for Sir Antoin, the viscount. The work is challenging but rewarding, and evidently much admired by my hosts. Nobles have come from nearby estates to have their mounts fitted with our steel.

I have today crafted a bit for a hippogriff. Your notes were a great help, but even so, I nearly lost a finger to the beast; no wonder they must be trained from birth, or that they make such fearsome war mounts. Such nobility in a creature, Master! The first bit, a darkened steel of my own design, was cleft in two by the powerful beak. I had to use a hardened ported-curb bit. I was pleased with the final result.

Yours,
Mattias

Master,

I was roused before dawn. Sir Antoin and a dozen retainers rode out to the nearby forest of Ansienne, bidding me join them. A temporary forge was already glowing white hot in a clearing some way into the trees. I dismounted and took my station by the anvil, laying out my tools.

The viscount told me to avert my gaze. I refused, for I am not easily cowed, but he insisted. I would have stood my ground, but a call echoed through the sun-touched branches such as I have never heard: neither quite avian nor equine. I dropped my eyes to the ground. Something landed behind me in the clearing. Its breath played on my neck as it approached. Antoin backed away, eying whatever stood behind me. I set to work.

Although I saw portions of the peryton – many-hued feathers, small but powerful wings, razor sharp fangs and talons – I dared not look upon the entire creature. The beast stood about 14 hands high by my estimation, and took both the bit and the saddle well enough, although not without several reheats and fittings. I sensed it was impatient, but knew that it must suffer my touch. In time, the work was completed, and only a sense of emptiness told me the peryton had left silently upon those feathered wings.

Lord Antoin nodded at me; I think he was pleased. I asked him how such a mature beast could be tamed. He was less than forthcoming, but it would appear that the peryton chooses its rider. I can only guess at its criteria.

Mattias

Gerond,

Today the Damsel arrived. The pegasus was a simple matter – I fashioned the bit from kiln-baked iron-wood, and the saddle-tree was a light-twisted narrow-brace. The beast stood and moved without command as I worked, as though reading my mind. I had encountered such mounts during my time at the capital, and mentioned the nature of the pegasus' capture to my host. He scoffed at my naivete and brusquely explained that while other nations might trap pegasi, in Equitaine they are bred – most famously in the western hills by the Whitewing ordo.

Yesterday, after the noble pegasus, I was set to simple shoeing of the castle's mounts. An insult to one of my skills, but under the circumstances, welcome relief. I worked on many breeds, from great draft horses that pull the siege trains with feet like dining plates, to nimble mountain ponies with tiny, gnarled hooves – hardy creatures indeed.

Matthias

I am summoned. I am to be taken to a mysterious creature for another fitting. The knights and servants are more tense and secretive than ever. From my aperture I can see a covered wagon the size of a steam tank. I believe it contains water; damp seeps from the vehicle. A ring of knights surround it, swords drawn. Something is moving inside, vigorously rocking the wagon.

Lord Antoin and several men, fully armoured by the sound, are at my door. I hear low snatches of conversation: "fey steed" and – a fearful breath – *"nuckelavee"*.

Now my skill is to be truly tested.

M

—Letters held in the archives of the Guild of Farriers

FEY

Brandon of the Briars would tell stories. He was a famous brigand, true, but he was a boy once. He grew up in Linsignes, and would spend the winter days in the lord's keep with the other children of the castle's town, that being the custom in the northern realms. He would sit and listen to the fireside tales of old Carys the washerwoman, and never would he forget a single one.

He would learn the stories of the five Fey Paramount, who served in the Queen's Court. The Green Knight was the first and greatest of them, who taught Uther to be a knight, and is said to have forged the First Sword. Daemons and dark fey alike could not stand before him, and when we are in direst need, the Lady sends him to aid those of true heart. His gifts to us now and always are the Principles of the knights.

The Snow Childe came next in the tellings. With her beautiful haunting blue eyes and pale skin, she playfully commands the winds, but her tantrums create the winter storms. The Queen of Cups, in Her mercy to us, keeps the Childe in court, letting her out only after the harvest times. Sometimes though, she escapes, like all mischievous children do, and brings the storms and snows too early to the realm. In the North, they keep the hearths ever lit, and leave out sweets for her to keep the storms at bay, and gifts are given to children in her honour.

The Third is the Hooded Man, who speaks in whispers, and in ages past taught us to hunt and the secrets of taming beasts. Indeed, he can tame any creature, and young brides pray to him to subdue their husbands: for what wilder beast is there than man? He can coax any beast to serve him, and from any instrument a tune, and he is honoured by high and low alike in every hunter's hut or feasting hall.

Next comes the Lord of the Sea, a mighty merman with a hundred mermaid brides. He is The Evermaiden's ally, sworn to come to her aid, and out of courtesy guard Her people's ships. Be warned though, the Lord of the Sea is a fickle fey, and capricious. Should you cause him the slightest insult, he can send mighty waves to swallow ships to the cold depths below.

Finally comes the Beldame, the wise old woman, who comes to us in our dotage and takes us in our time to the Queen's Court to be judged for our lives gone by. She gives us advice and comfort, she tells us tales and secrets the living aren't meant to know, and all the wise heed her words, for of all the fey, she knows the Lady's heart best.

Beyond the Five, Brandon learned also of many others who serve Her interests; some sent to aid us, Her people of Equitaine, and others for stranger reasons few can fathom, as Brandon himself would attest.

But more than this, Brandon of the Briars would come to know all the tales he could find, from the tricks played by Karde to the brave deeds of Uther. Great heroes, the Sainted, and all the fey from noblest unicorn to the most terrifying kelpie or the smallest sprite would enrapture him. He would listen under the Kissing Tree when the other children were at play, and would sit at the feet of every minstrel, fool, or bard who would tell a tale. Who can know how many stories he came to memorise. Perhaps a hundred hundred or more – and they would all come to serve him when he left his home.

He is remembered as a great trickster himself, and as many stories are told about him now as the stories he learned in his youth. He travelled to distant lands to atone for many mischiefs, only to come home to our sweet realm and immerse himself once again in schemes and troubles.

He sought out Oob, the greatest of the naiads, for her help in wooing the beautiful maid Bethany. The ordo of our Sisters of Sincerity which tended to stone and stream, but took solemn vows of chastity did not look kindly on his advances. He stole the blue flower from Averi, the Fey Knight. Lord of many fey, and keeper of many enchantments, his flower was beautiful, but moreover could mend any sickness to rights. He saved the questing knight Geoffroy of Ouestfleur from the dread Carcole, a foul snail larger than two riders abreast, its slime both caustic and acidic. He befriended the Matagot Mireille when he saved her from the Guivre. A strange fey whose form was a mix of cat and fox, and her charms would save Brandon many a time.

He fought against robber knights who had forsaken their vows. False knights, these, who had turned to banditry after committing the great sin of cowardice and not seeking atonement in quest or penance. He claimed to have met and rendered aid to the last of the Quin, a secret ordo given to worship of the great Trickster, and saved them from extinction. Though never undertaking the Quest personally, he served with the penitent in battle and through many hardships. He would live as an outlaw, but also as an honoured guest in many a court throughout his years.

In this compendium, we seek to bring the greatest of his stories, many no doubt allegorical, together in one place. They lie twixt myth and history, but we sense there is great truth in them. Be they at court or war camp, when fey come to honour our alliances and mutual faith in the Lady Beyond, many still remember Brandon and invoke his name.

In fact, some which grace these pages can still be met when the horns of war are called. If you should encounter a naiad or a sylph, remember the courtesies described in such tales, for they will serve you and see you prosper. Heroes like Brandon were and are a bridge between us, and the wise would do well to ever heed the lessons herein.

May these tales serve both to teach and to entertain, just as old Carys' did for our Brandon.

Your Obedient Servant,
Odo de Goulton

—Foreword to Brandon of the Briars, a collection of Northern Tales

Compatible with
IX
AGE
TM
The 9th Age™

THE IX AGE
FANTASY BATTLES

Gather close, ye who would learn of the strange peoples and wondrous places of the Ninth Age. None of us can know the secrets of the entire world, but if you seek a little wisdom on a particular culture or nation, open up this tome and discover what there is to tell.

So you wish for tales of chivalry? Very well, you shall know of gleaming armour and lowered lance. Some call it the fairest of realms, but remember: Equitaine was born in darkness, and many a traveler has never returned from that mysterious land.